Samuel Jennings

My Visit to the Goldfields in the Southeast Wynaad

Samuel Jennings

My Visit to the Goldfields in the Southeast Wynaad

ISBN/EAN: 9783743383852

Manufactured in Europe, USA, Canada, Australia, Japa

Cover: Foto ©Andreas Hilbeck / pixelio.de

Manufactured and distributed by brebook publishing software
(www.brebook.com)

Samuel Jennings

My Visit to the Goldfields in the Southeast Wynaad

MY VISIT TO THE GOLDFIELDS

SOUTH-EAST WYNAAD.

a

ON THE COONOR GHAT.

MY VISIT TO THE GOLDFIELDS

IN THE

SOUTH-EAST WYNAAD.

BY

SAMUEL JENNINGS, F.L.S., F.R.G.S.,

SECRETARY TO THE SOUTH INDIAN GOLD MINING COMPANY, AND THE
INDIAN GLENROCK GOLD MINING COMPANY (LIMITED).

LONDON:

CHAPMAN AND HALL, LIMITED,

HENRIETTA STREET, COVENT GARDEN.

1881.

PRINTED BY WILLIAM CLOWES AND SONS, LIMITED, LONDON AND BECCLES.

PREFACE.

———◆———

THE writer of the following pages had no idea whatever that, upon his return from a recent official visit to the goldfields, he would be called upon to write a book. Possibly, had he anticipated such a task, this volume would have been somewhat different. The information afforded might have been more general, and touched the interests, operations, and prospects of other companies besides those upon which he had been instructed to report.

This little volume is, therefore, no more than a slight sketch of his own personal experiences. Enlivened with engravings from drawings made upon the spot, its object is to familiarize the English reader with the country in which such great results will, in all probability, soon be achieved. It will, perhaps, be interesting, hereafter, as a record of what the district

once was, before gold had so completely changed it
—as California, Colorado, and Australia have been
changed.

The writer has seen quite enough to convince him
that the South-East Wynaad is a rich auriferous
district. Time and experience will show to what
extent profitable returns may be expected; for actual
results we anxiously wait.

He is also able to testify that vigorous operations
are being carried on upon some estates; that tunnels
are being driven, machinery erected, roads made,
bungalows, coolie lines, and stores are springing up
in all directions—the evidences of energetic deter-
mination to accomplish whatever is to be accomplished.

Experienced and capable skill is to be found there
also: and not a little enthusiasm amongst mining
engineers, who to a man are confident, so far as the
writer has met with them. Not a single word of
discouragement did he hear throughout the whole of
his stay in the country. The croakers are not to be
found amongst men who have seen the place. If
we want them we must look here in England, where
it can scarcely be believed that we have been so long
in India and failed to discover the hidden treasure.
Without a shadow of doubt there is gold in plenty;

the work before us is to **extract the precious metal** from its matrix. Concerning this most important matter a few remarks have been added—not by way of indicating how it is to be done in India, but for the purpose of warning those interested, that it is yet to be decided how best to accomplish this desirable end. Science and intelligence will, doubtless, solve the question sooner or later; but full results can scarcely be hoped for so early as the more sanguine expect; though even upon the first rough crushings a satisfactory return will, in all probability, be obtained. Whatever that return may be—when the time comes, it will certainly be considerably *less* than what may subsequently be accomplished, when the best method of treating the concentrates shall have been determined.

A dozen photographic negatives were brought to England by the author, prints from which may be obtained on application to the London Stereoscopic Company, Cheapside.

CONTENTS.

CHAPTER I.

FROM BOMBAY TO THE WYNAAD.

CHAPTER II.

OUR "SOUTH INDIAN" ESTATE.

CHAPTER III.

OUR "GLENROCK" ESTATE.

CHAPTER VIII.

THE PROCESS OF REDUCTION.

CHAPTER IX.

A FINAL WORD.

ILLUSTRATIONS.

MY VISIT TO THE GOLDFIELDS.

CHAPTER I.

FROM BOMBAY TO THE WYNAAD.

A quick voyage—Reason of my visit explained—Two routes to the Wynaad—A choking railway journey—Aspect of the country—Mattapollium and its hotel—The dâk mail—How about luggage ?—A dangerous drive—Coonoor—A beautiful spot—Hurried off—Sanatorium of Wellington—A change of climate indeed !—Ootacamund—Australian trees—The road to the Wynaad—I look for gold, and find coffee—Appearance of the plains of Wynaad—In doubt as to the road—The Balcarres Valley—A neglected nugget—I meet my friend, and reach my destination.

In commencing this brief account of my trip to India, I must put aside one strong temptation—the desire to describe the first portion of it, the voyage out. But I will not risk boring the reader by re-telling a twice-told tale. It must suffice, therefore, to say, that I had a pleasant time of it, with pleasant companions, on board one of the time-honoured P. and O. boats. On the seventeenth day after leaving London, I landed in Bombay ; a very different affair from the tedious voyage in the palmy days of John Company.

My destination was the Wynaad goldfields, of which so much has been said and written. I had resolved to see them for myself, and to report the result of my visit to those who were interested in furthering the new industry. It must not be supposed for a moment that I was sent to " prospect," as it is termed, with the view of forming any new company. My commission was a very simple one, if it were one that required both careful observation, patient inquiry, and some knowledge of organization. I had no intention to paint, either in bright or in gloomy colours, the prospects of the gold companies already in the field. The primary object of my journey, was to organize the staff, to introduce a proper system of accounts, and to initiate various improvements in local arrangements, with a view to secure both greater efficiency and more accurate and speedy information on a variety of matters of importance. Besides this, I was instructed to report generally upon things as I found them, more especially as regards the companies with which I am officially connected. I had no interest to serve, by misrepresentation or exaggeration. The following description of what I saw and did is, therefore, a simple record of the impressions left on my mind by the journey; and in so much, can claim, I hope, the confidence of my readers in respect to its trustworthiness.

I landed, as I have said, at Bombay; from which

city I found that the Wynaad can be reached by
two routes. One is by the British-India Company's
coasting steamers to Calicut—a voyage of three or four
days, dependent on the number of intermediate ports
touched at; and from Calicut by road through the
Malabar District, either to the Tambracherry or the
Carcoor Ghât. This latter portion, a distance of
seventy miles, is accomplished in a bullock cart or
bandy, and takes another two days. The other route
is to go by rail to Madras, and thence to Mattapollium on the Madras Railway; and by mail tonga
to Ootacamund. This is three days' journey from
Bombay, including twelve hours which must be spent
in Madras. From Ootacamund the traveller may
ride into the Wynaad in eight or ten hours, as the
case may be.

For various reasons I selected the latter route,
leaving Bombay at two o'clock on a Wednesday,
reaching Madras at six on Friday morning, leaving
again at six the same evening, and arriving at
Mattapollium at 10.30 on Saturday morning, and
at Ootacamund at four in the afternoon. It is pleasant enough travelling by rail in India in the cold
weather; but with an atmosphere of choking dust,
and the thermometer registering over 90° in the
carriage, with the blinding sunlight in the daytime, and
not unfrequently at night a chilly wind, such a journey
is no ordinary trial of endurance. One could have
borne it better, no doubt, had there been any redeem-

ing quality in the character of the scenery. But this may simply be described as featureless; for, after leaving the mountainous approach to Poonah, it is all a dead level, dry and uninteresting. The same may be said, in a measure, of the country through which the Madras Railway passes, except, indeed, that everything wears a thoroughly tropical appearance; the aridity of Central India giving place to the verdure of the south; whilst distant hills occasionally break the monotony of the general level of the plain.

At Pothanoor Junction, 302 miles from Madras, we left the main line, which touches the western coast at Beypore. A short branch, some twenty miles in length, passing through Coimbatore, a rather important town, terminates at Mattapollium, six miles from the foot of the Neilgherri Hills.

It is always advisable to arrange beforehand for a seat in one of the mail tongas, or carts. This may be accomplished by telegraphing to the agent of the Tonga Dâk Company at Ootacamund, informing him of the train by which you will arrive. It is well to do this, for it will prevent the possibility of an unpleasant detention in this miserable village. I should, however, admit that there certainly is an hotel at Mattapollium; but I never heard of any one patronizing it except in a case of the direst necessity.

The mail tonga, in which the next thirty-five miles to Ootacamund is done, is a strongly built vehicle on

two wheels, with low axles. It accommodates three
passengers; one by the side of the driver, the other
two behind, as in our dogcarts. The pole passes
through the body, and is furnished with an iron yoke
that rests upon the collars of the horses. Within a
quarter of an hour after the arrival of the train, the
mail-bags have been stowed away and a start is
made. If there be room, some of your luggage will
accompany you; if not, you must do as best you
can. In any event, if you have much, the bulk of it
must follow you—I need not say at more than an
appreciable distance—borne on the heads of coolies.

But we are off. The horn tootles as though we
were leaving the White Horse Cellar, Piccadilly, and
away we go at full gallop, through the bazaar and
over a bridge crossing the Bhowany river; in the
bed of which, by the way, the natives frequently
wash for gold. This crossed, a straight road of six
miles, shaded by large trees, brought us to the first
place for a change of horses. This is Kullar, at the
foot of the Coonoor Ghât; and here the ascent com-
mences.

The scenery increases in interest, as we proceed at
a flying pace up the zigzag roads. The route here
has also the element of a little peril. Danger does
not seem to enter into the coachman's calculation.
Whisking round the sharp corners, skirting the very
edge of steep precipices, escaping as by a miracle the
stone posts protecting the wooden bridges that cross

the mountain torrents, checked for a moment by trains of heavily laden bullock waggons and bandies that laboriously toil up the steep incline, and often running perilously near utter ruin from collision with carriages on the downward journey, the drive, it will be allowed, is exciting in its way.

Sixteen miles from Kullar, the beautiful station of Coonoor, 6500 feet above the sea, is reached. It boasts a picturesque waterfall, foaming over high boulders of rock, deep down into a thickly wooded valley. I have visited several of the hill stations in Upper India, but not one of them appeared to me so charming as this. The beauty of the foliage, the rich deep green of the grass, the fine outlines of the surrounding mountains, the calm surface of the artificial lake, the pretty residences nestling amongst the trees on the hillsides, the varied hues of the trees and shrubs grouped in the hollows, the brilliant crimson of the rhododendron bloom, and the rich colours—browns, yellows, and reds—of the young leaves of some of the trees, form altogether a charming whole. It is a natural picture, in contemplation of which one would fain linger. But it is not to be. The driver has a stern sense of duty; and with a fresh tootling of the horn and cracking of the whip, we hurry away past the Military Sanatorium of Wellington, a handsome pile of barracks some two miles beyond. With its well-kept roads, smooth turf, and noble eucalyptus trees—the blue gum of

Australia, which thrives in these hills amazingly well —this establishment seems to achieve all that is desirable in a place of the kind. Some nine miles more bring us to Ootacamund, the end of our day's journey.

The first thing to strike one on arrival, was the extraordinary contrast with the climate we had left behind us in the morning. Here we were 7500 to 8000 feet above the sea, in a fresh and exhilarating atmosphere. I ought, in truth, to have looked for a change of the kind; for I had been duly warned that before the day closed, I should want wraps and rugs. But the advice seemed absurd in the sultry heat of the plains; yet an overcoat would not have been unpleasant during the last hour of our drive.

Ootacamund is the summer residence of the Government of Madras. It is therefore an important station, and covers a considerable area. There are shops at which almost anything can be procured. It also has a very good hotel, an excellent club-house, library, churches, and other public buildings. The main feature of the place, however, is its lake. It is seven miles in circumference, enclosed on all sides by lofty hills with rounded summits, extensively planted with various Australian trees. The general aspect of the place is, however, much marred by squalid native huts and a dirty bazaar. There is a considerable native population, with all the usual unsightly accompaniments; and these, it need not be added, go a long way to spoil the beauty of what might be a very lovely and lovable spot.

But in spite of these trifling drawbacks, it must be admitted that Ootacamund is a charming place. The air is so invigorating that, in truth, it is not unusual for visitors to feel a little inconvenienced, at first, from its rarity. For this often produces sleeplessness at night, which, however, soon passes away; and once acclimatized, the sickly dwellers in the plains are not long in picking up health and vigour. Indeed, a few days up here in the clouds will effect a cure.

The journey from Ootacamund to the Wynaad is beyond the usual route of the mail dâk, and must be specially arranged. A horseman acquainted with all the short cuts, can accomplish the distance in six or seven hours; although, by the road, it would occupy considerably more time. In my case, a carriage had been provided to take me as far as Neddiwattum, twenty-one miles to the north-west. Starting at eight o'clock in the morning, with three changes of horses, I reached the rough but convenient hotel about eleven.

The country is undulating and grassy, bare of timber except in such hollow places as afford the necessary moisture and shelter. In these spots there are lovely groups of trees, and often a delicious undergrowth of ferns—veritable oases in a desert of

uninteresting slopes, covered at this season with
burnt-up grass. In the immediate vicinity of Neddiwattum the scene changes, and after passing the
highest point, the road descends through rich forest
towards the western edge of the lofty Neilgherri
range.

At the hotel I found a horse awaiting me; and,
after a tolerable breakfast, I started on the last stage
of my journey.

The first mile or so, was through the valuable
cinchona plantation belonging to Government. The
trees were about twenty feet in height; they had
been barked, and the stems were carefully protected
with a covering of bast. After passing the plantation, a magnificent panorama opens out. Three
thousand feet below, extending as far as the eye
can reach, the wide expanse of country extending
from Mysore on the right, all over the Wynaad to
the distant mountains beyond Nellumboor, and
bounded on the left by the Neilgherris beyond the
Ochterlony Valley, lies before me. This was my first
introduction to the gold region, of which so much
has recently been said. One peculiarity struck me.
The whole country seems broken up into countless
undulations—tumbled, as it were, like the waves of
the ocean. Through the centre of this, rises a higher
ridge, of which Needlerock Peak is the most striking
feature. Towards the north, the plateau seems a
vast expanse of forest, but the Wynaad is not so

thickly wooded. To the south there is a further steep descent to the plains.

From Neddiwattum to Gudalur, the native town close under my feet in the Wynaad tableland, it is nine miles by the road, which zigzags down the face of the steep declivity. This distance may be reduced to five miles by following the bridle-path—a precipitous and rocky track, along which careful riding is an absolute necessity. Gudalur is some 2600 feet above the sea. About a mile beyond the bazaar, the road branches. Here I had some difficulty in finding out which direction to take. Luckily I discovered a native who could speak Hindustani; and from him I learned that the road to the right would take me to Nellialum, the left leading to Devala. The latter was my route; so for twelve miles more I followed its course, winding through a rich, hilly, and well-wooded country. I passed Seeputty, and knew I was at last on one of the estates of the Indian Gold Mines Company, and that the Alpha mine was not far off. I might, indeed, expect to see evidences before long of mining activity. But it proved that I expected too much; for I saw nothing but coffee plantations.

At Devala there is a good hotel. It has besides a few bungalows and a native bazaar; but I had still five miles further to ride. The road now became much more interesting, skirting as it does the very edge of the magnificent valleys that form the approaches to the Wynaad from the plains. In particular I was enchanted with the fine view down the Balcarres Valley, so full of noble timber.*

Here I was glad to meet my good friend Harvey, who had ridden out to welcome me; and as we had plenty to say on topics of mutual interest, the rest of my long ride went by quickly and pleasantly. After passing through the Richmond estate, we crossed the only bit of level country I had seen.

"A swamp in the rains," said Harvey.

"Then a bad look-out for the future city of Pundalur," said I.

"Yes; that is Hadiabetta Peak. Glenrock lies on the other side of those hills."

We leave them on our left, and ride through Rosedell, belonging to the Phœnix Company. Then we enter St. Thomé; coffee again. At last we are on South Indian property, and I congratulate myself on having arrived at my journey's end.

"Not yet," replied Harvey; "you have more than a mile to go yet."

---

* This is a grand estate, concerning which, if I am not much mistaken, the public will hear again before long. An attempt was made, some eighteen months ago, to raise the necessary capital for working it; but the scheme fell through. It was born before due time. I could not obtain any information as to the proprietor's views for opening out this property; but was informed that some of the richest reefs in the Wynaad were known to run through the Balcarres Valley, and that a veritable nugget, of the kind that Australians know all about, was actually picked up when I was there.

What interminable loops the road takes! So long a way round, and so short a distance across! The valley below is all filled with coffee. Then we pass Mr. Wright's bungalow—more coffee; then some jungle and scrub; and a side path ascending a big hill; and up, up we go, higher and higher, till we reach the summit, and there find ourselves at home at the Mango-Tree Bungalow, 4000 feet above the sea. Darkness had already set in; dinner was almost ready, and, for it, I was *quite* ready; and the long night's rest which followed the hospitable meal, was a grateful end to my first day in the Wynaad.

NOTE.—Since writing the above, the Indian Consolidated Gold Company has been formed to work the whole of these fine estates, extending all the way from Devala to Pundalur, and possessing some of the richest reefs in the district. I have seen quartz from them with visible gold in it.

CHAPTER II.

OUR "SOUTH INDIAN" ESTATE.

Reception by my new comrades—Plans for the future—Views from the Mango-Tree Bungalow—Heaps of quartz and their attraction —The dynamite mine—A colony of spiders—The outcrops on No. 1 Reef—Boulders and the true reef—How mistakes are made—Our four tunnels on No. 1 Reef—Another brace of tunnels—Condition of the work and prospects of production—. The character of the quartz—Free gold—Experiences at the St. John del Rey mine—The result of assays—Australian experiences of result and cost—What we may look for—Exceptional bearings of our reefs—Possibilities of the future.

I WAS up early on the morning of the next day, which I had purposed to devote strictly to business ; and when that was got through, to the arrangement of some plan for expeditions to the various points of interest connected with the operations of our companies. I received, I need scarcely say, a most hearty welcome from every member of the staff. My visit evidently afforded great satisfaction, for through it their main difficulties would be so much better understood, and their efforts to overcome them appreciated. For my own part, I should see for myself; and thus, on my return, be able to explain a

host of things that could never be made clear by
writing. In this manner incorrect impressions would
be removed. This feeling my new comrades shared
with me.

These expressions of good feeling were very pleasant. They caused me to enter upon the duties of
my mission with a consciousness that all concerned,
directors, proprietors, and employés, must derive
benefit in more ways than one from the results of my
visit to the properties.

The site of Mango-Tree Bungalow, the mining
captain's quarters, had been admirably chosen. It
commands the whole sweep of country round, and is
close to the main operations of the South Indian
Company. Facing the south-west, on the left, is the
high ridge of the Devala Moyar estate. Nearer
again, the eye glances over "Richmond," "Rosedell," St. Thomé: a series of rounded hills; whilst
towering right in front rises the bluff head of Hadiabetta, the south-eastern side of the Glenrock Valley
receding in the distance. The eye irresistibly followed
the course of these far-off gently swelling plains to
the sea, seventy miles away. On the right, above
the opposite slope of the valley, is the tableland of
Wentworth, and the country towards Cherambadi.
This is about the same general level as our property,
though it is broken up in a perfect sea of hills, and
is set off by a background of the cloud-capped peaks
of the Velery Mulla range of mountains. These

NEEDLE ROCK, FROM MANGO TREE.

push themselves some thirty or forty miles forward into the plain, their highest points being 8000 feet above the sea.

To the north, a lofty range of hills shuts out the distant view ; but close below are the great heaps of quartz, indicating the entrances to the levels driven into the hillside to intersect the auriferous reefs. To the eastward, we look over the South Indian estates, beyond Bittusal, away to Athikanu and Trevelyan, and the remarkable Needlerock Peak. The latter rises conelike above the surrounding hills. The far distance is canopied, as it were, by the blue heights of the Neilgherris. The whole, in truth, makes one magnificent panorama, which embraces nearly all the most interesting and best-known gold-mining sites. It is true that we cannot see the estates of the Glasgow Company. Alpha, Ham-slade, and those in the immediate neighbourhood of Devala, are hidden by the forest-crowned range of hills on the Devala Moyar Company's property ; whilst Tambracherry is thirty miles away to the westward.

I have mentioned some heaps of quartz. These, it may be believed, were sure to be the first attraction ; and I was soon descending the Bungalow Hill with Captain Gifford, to make a closer acquaintance with the scene of his skill and labour. At the foot of the declivity the path turns off to the left. As we skirted the hill for a few hundred yards, we observed the dynamite magazine; very properly sunk into the hillside in such a manner that a possible explosion could do but little damage. I should perhaps say that the caps are kept in store away from the dynamite.

Whilst examining the magazine, my curiosity was aroused by seeing the corners of the trench in which the hut was built, covered with a mass of something black, woolly or hairy—what could it be? On close inspection, it proved to be an enormous colony of long-legged spiders, huddled together in an extraordinary manner. A small stone thrown at them caused the lot to fall down in masses; and in a few moments the whole place was alive with spiders crawling in every direction. They appeared to be full grown, not recently hatched. I had often before watched the habits of various species of Indian spiders, but had never seen so vast a number huddled together as in this case.

In front of the magazine, a few planks led us across to the face of the opposite hill, up which we ascend, through scrub and dwarf trees, till we arrive at the entrance of No. 1 Tunnel. This is forty-eight feet below the summit of the hill, where large boulders of quartz form the outcrop of what is called No. 1 Reef. Forty-eight feet have been driven east and west at this point.

The direction of a reef, I should here say, is ascertained by observing the line of outcrops on the surface; but its dip can only be discovered by driving levels to intersect it at depth. In fact, no so-called reef can be properly said to have been proved until such levels have been driven, or shafts sunk upon it. Nothing can be more deceptive than some of these heaps of quartz boulders, particularly those found on low ground. They may prove on examination to be no more than enormous masses of stone, detached ages ago from a reef, and carried to their present situation by some tremendous convulsion of nature, and subsequently, and by degrees, partly buried in the earth. There are examples in the Wynaad of the fall of a reef, and the consequent scattering of its fragments all over the adjacent country. It is needless to say that mining operations upon such detached boulders will result in nothing but disappointment.

It is, I should observe, in determining the direction and the dip of a true reef, that the skill and experience of the mining engineer are called into play. Mistakes, in truth, may very easily be made. There is an example of this on the very hill we are now exploring. Near the summit and close to the outcrops, is an abandoned shaft, which had been sunk some two years ago to a depth of about forty feet. It had, however, been started on the wrong side of the dip. The deeper they went, the further the reef receded from them; and the search was given up in the belief that there was no reef here after

c

all. Captain Gifford's operations have proved that
his predecessor was wrong. Indeed, when once the
thing itself is seen, the method or reason upon which
this fine reef has been opened out is simplicity itself.

Sixty feet below No. 1 Tunnel, we came upon the
entrance to No. 2. This has been driven twenty-five
feet into the hillside, where the reef, which proved
to be eight feet in thickness, was again reached.
Some fifty-eight feet have been exposed along its
course.

The third tunnel, more to the westward, is seventy
feet below No. 2, and the reef here proved to be
fifty-seven feet from the entrance, and is twelve feet
thick. Here, again, driving has been carried for a
distance of thirty-seven feet along the reef. The
deepest tunnel of all is No. 4, at the foot of the hill,
only ten feet below No. 3, and ninety feet to the
west. At this spot the reef was reached at a distance
of fifty-four feet. This tunnel is 180 feet below the
outcrops on the hill. Consequently, it is certain that
there is a wall of quartz over our heads, when standing in this tunnel, no less than 180 feet high. How
much lies below our feet, who can tell!

Ascending the hill, and passing round its western
extremity, a second branch of the same range is
reached. Into this two more tunnels have been
driven, Nos. 5 and 6. These were directed towards
another series of outcrops, indicating the presence
of a reef having very nearly the same bearing

as that already described; and, as a matter of fact, these levels proved the assumption to have been correct. No. 5 has been driven a distance of 110 feet, and has passed through a small vein of quartz, but has not yet reached No. 2 Reef. No. 6 also intersected several thin branches, and at a distance of 192 feet reached the reef, which is very massive—fully six feet in width, and highly impregnated with iron and arsenical pyrites. Towards the west the reef increases in size, and looks very well.

We have, therefore, upon the South Indian Company's property, two well-defined reefs, both of which have been proved at depth, and found to consist of gold-bearing quartz. No. 1, as I have shown, has been reached at four points, and No. 2 at one, with another point not far off still to be developed. From all the five proved exits, an abundant supply of quartz can be poured forth as fast as it may be wanted for the reduction works. The tunnels all are well excavated. The walls are clean and smooth; the roofs are arched and about seven feet high. Great heaps of quartz are piled outside the entrances, and plenty more stored away inside, ready for removal when required.

Then as to the character of the quartz. On this point my opinion must necessarily be formed upon the reports given by others, who are better qualified to speak on such a technical subject. The quartz is very white; stained pretty freely with a reddish tinge,

and moderately charged with *pyrites*—a metallic combination of iron, arsenic, sulphur, silver, and gold.
The presence of copper also is indicated.   Free gold
—that is, gold uncombined with other metals—is but
seldom met with.   When it is found, it is found, as a
rule, in quartz near the surface, where atmospheric
influence has been brought to bear upon the metallic
deposits in the stone.   Decomposition then sets in,
and the metals subject to oxidation having become
resolved, the precious metals, which are unaffected
by the atmosphere, remain as granular or *flaky* or
filmy deposits in the crevices of the rotten and honey-
combed quartz, which is called *gozzan*.*

Captain Gifford very frequently crushes the quartz
taken from these tunnels, and states that after
having washed it, he almost invariably obtains colour,
or a few specks of gold; quite enough to establish
the auriferous character of these reefs.   But assays
of samples will always vary considerably, and can
never be relied upon to indicate with any certainty
how much profit may be calculated upon.   Working

* This is the general character of the quartz in this neighbourhood, but there is a probability that true fissure veins may be
reached at greater depth, where the gold has come up from below
unmixed with pyrites.   If so, it will obviously in this condition be
much more easily recovered than from pyritous quartz.   Where
the gold is free, simple stamping and washing will suffice; but the
amalgamating process is very tedious, and the risk of loss is greater.
Thus, with the St. John del Réy Company, which has been working
on a kind of pyritous ore for many years, with great success, there
is still a certain percentage of loss which is ascertained by a
careful analysis of the tailings.

in bulk alone can demonstrate the true value of the reef as a whole; and even then, I strongly suspect that variations in richness will be met with. Nevertheless, if, as Australian experts tell us, an average yield of three pennyweights to the ton of quartz * will pay expenses, our shareholders have but little reason to fear the test of wholesale crushing. Judging from the various assays which from time to time have been made by independent authorities, there should be ample margin to cover even heavier working charges than occur in Australian mines, and a tolerably fair balance would still remain for dividends. This, at all events, is the freely expressed expectation of men on the spot, whose opinions are those of practical gold miners, experienced in Australia, Brazil, and California. More than this, I think, cannot reasonably be expected at the present stage of our operations.

Whilst on the subject of these two reefs, it will be interesting to observe how they have disproved a theory that has been advanced by more than one recognized authority. These have declared that all true auriferous reefs have a direction a little west of north and east of south. If this be the general rule, we have here two notable exceptions. The bearing of our reefs is a trifle north of west and south of east; and they can be traced for a considerable

---

* Three pennyweights is equal to 10s. 6d. the ton. Our gold is estimated to be worth from 70s. to 72s. the ounce.

distance across the properties. And it is more than probable that the reef at Bittusal, a mile and a quarter to the east, is a continuation of that we have opened out near the Mango-Tree. If this should prove correct, I leave my readers to calculate how long it will take to exhaust this enormous supply; even supposing that no fresh reefs can be discovered on their estates. Yet there are at least two other distinct reefs to the south of Bungalow Hill, where very significant outcrops may be easily traced. Their nature will be ascertained in course of driving a deep adit that has been recently commenced on the opposite side of a lofty hill that shuts off the South Indian from the Glenrock property.

CHAPTER III.

OUR " GLENROCK " ESTATE.

The road to Glenrock—The effects of heavy traffic—The bungalows
and outhouses—A cookshop in danger—The captain's home—A
splendid outlook—Preparations—A busy scene—A native contractor's stupidity—Precautions against delay—Nature of the
mining operations at Glenrock—Vestiges of old world mining
—A tunnel falls in—Native invocations—Work being done—
Auriferous nature of the ground—The tunnels and working
described.

THE reader will be certain that I paid a visit to
Glenrock on the earliest opportunity. Riding back
a distance of two miles over the road by which we
had first arrived, a bridle-path to the right is reached,
which cuts off a corner and brings one into the road
from Pundalur to Glenrock. From this point the
bazaar is visible at a considerable distance below
and partly sheltered by trees. The road appears to
have been much cut up by the constant passage of
heavily laden bandies, that for a month or six weeks
past have been bringing up the machinery from
Calicut. Indeed, on the day of my first visit, and
often subsequently, there was quite a block of
waggons passing up and down.

Winding round the hillsides, and continually ascending, we pass Mr. Ryan's bungalow on the left. It is noticeable here that the hill upon which it is built is planted with tea, whilst immediately above is the bluff-head of Hadiabetta Peak, its rocky precipitous face towards Glenrock, its rounded summit and steeply sloping grassy sides descending into the Phœnix Valley. On the right is another lofty hill, called Chic Hadiabetta. Upon a spur of this, high above the road, are the two Glenrock bungalows, reached by a steep path. The first of them is occupied by the English miners and smiths. It is intended to accommodate four men. It has a central dining and sitting room, and two private rooms on either side; whilst a verandah, ever welcome in this country, extends the entire length of the building. The cook-house runs on one side. Curiously, and I must say unaccountably, the entrance to a tunnel is being driven behind the latter building. The intention is to ascertain if the outcrops of quartz on the hill above indicate a reef. If this be the case, I fancy the cook-house will be found to be rather in the way.

A little further along this advanced plateau, and commanding a magnificent view of the whole extent of the Glenrock Valley, stands the mining captain's bungalow. Not many residences can boast of such a prospect. To the right, the steep sides of mountain are covered with dense forest; beyond which, across the valley and perched up amongst the hills, our

Mango-Tree Bungalow can be seen, more than a mile off as the crow flies. On the opposite side are the coffee plantations of Glenrosa; and extending in front and far away to the left, are the northern slopes of the Glenrock Valley, with the rugged and picturesque Velery Mulla Mountains for a background. Immediately below the bungalow there is a precipitous descent to an undulating platform, planted all over with coffee. Beyond this, again, another slope, thickly wooded, completely hides the river—some fifteen hundred feet below. To the left is the range of hills forming the boundary between the Glenrock and the Phœnix estates, the sides of which beyond the coffee are covered with thick forest. Such are the general features of the Glenrock estate, which comprises 3100 acres, of which 420 are under coffee cultivation, and about 2000 under timber.

Descending from the bungalows, and resuming our ride along the main road, we shortly arrived at the corrugated iron store, where a busy scene was presented. Here the men—both Europeans and natives—were engaged in arranging and housing the more delicate parts of the stamping machinery, to be erected down in the valley as soon as the site has been prepared and the connecting road finished. Captain Hambley, the engineer in charge, is superintending this part of the work. For a considerable distance the road is lined with iron pipes, cog-wheels, anvils, stamp heads, sheets, rails, barrels, and cases, and the cry is, " Still they come."

Before I left, the sling waggons and trollies had arrived, bringing up some of the heavier pieces. These had been delayed on the road by one of those unfortunate occurrences which, added to native stupidity, so often make the best-laid plans gang a-aglee, whether they be laid by mice or by men. A native contractor had engaged to bring these heavy loads up from Calicut through the Carcoor Ghât, and had actually got as far as Nadukani, four-fifths of the journey, when his bullocks were attacked by cattle disease, and some of them died on the road. Instead of sending a message on to the mines and asking for help, he became alarmed at the possible consequences to himself of the failure to deliver his freight, and returned with his remaining bullocks to Calicut, leaving the waggons on the road! As day after day passed and no news could be obtained of the expected machinery, a messenger was despatched down the ghât, who returned the next day only to tell our people that the waggons had been abandoned. Arrangements were accordingly made to bring them up ; and they arrived in due course without further mishap. Nevertheless time had been lost, and it was evidently no longer safe to trust, as heretofore, to the contract system. An officer was therefore appointed to accompany and manage future transports ; so that, in case of difficulty, intelligent assistance would at once be rendered, and thus the risk of loss of time avoided. There were still some sixteen or eighteen heavy pieces to be brought up; for which our specially constructed waggons had to return. But the roads and bridges having been put in proper repair, it was hoped that no further extraordinary delay would occur. Friendly aid, in the shape of the loan of waggons belonging to a neighbouring company, was cordially promised; and before the machinery can be really wanted for use, it will doubtless have all been safely delivered at the mines and properly erected.

Unlike the simplicity of the mining operations upon the South Indian property, those upon Glenrock appear to be attended with unusual difficulty. The character of the ground is totally different. Instead of a bare grassy rounded hill, as in the former, here we have a rugged, precipitous mountain-side, the surface of which is completely hidden by dense jungle and overshadowing trees. But there are abundant evidences of the extent to which this part of the property has been worked in ancient times : a sure proof of the existence of rich auriferous reefs not far below the surface. Deep shafts and open trenches are met with in all directions. Ages have elapsed since last they were scenes of mining activity; for huge trees have grown in these long since deserted works, and often they are completely hidden by the tangled mass of underwood.

These ancient shafts, endangering the safety of his own levels, are a source of considerable anxiety to the mining engineer. On one occasion, indeed, our men had a most narrow escape from being buried in their own tunnel, through striking into one of these hidden shafts. The loosened blocks of stone came rattling through the roof, and they had to run for their lives. They were fortunately able to secure the roof by strong timbering; and no further danger is apprehended.*

The mining operations upon Glenrock are directed upon two points. The main levels have been driven upon reefs showing upon the hill above and the hollow below the bungalow, and towards Chic Hadiabetta. Here, in one place, the reef shows plainly on the surface; a photograph, taken during my visit, is a capital illustration of the mode of working upon a reef. The other operations are being carried out on the opposite side of the valley, and high up the hill. This part of the property is called *Glenrosa*. Where the reef has been cut upon Glenrock, the quartz presents a different appearance to that on the South Indian property. The lode itself appears to be more slender, and split up into numerous branches. Captain Coward, who is in charge, spoke to me in very

* The effect of this averted danger on the native mind is, I should observe, rather curious. Such incidents are not looked upon as accidental. They are ascribed to the potent agency of some demon; and sacrifices are freely offered, to appease this supposed spirit and induce him to " move on."

MINERS' QUARTERS, GLENROCK.

hopeful terms of the whole appearance of the ground. "It was exactly," he said, "the same kind of ground as that which in Colorado is considered the most likely to contain gold in a workable condition. Indeed, it will be necessary here to examine all the soil and rock; for *not only is the quartz auriferous, but everything contiguous to it carries gold, even the clay and the gravel.* A hard close-grained *rock* showed, on assay, as much as two oz., three dwts. to the ton, and greenstone situated *under* the reef thirteen dwts." But not here alone is work now proceeding; for since I left the district, tunnels have been commenced upon two other likely spots, concerning which more will doubtless be heard before long.

Let me endeavour to give some idea of the nature and position of the various mining works on this part of the estate.

Commencing at the top of the hill above the bungalow, several open shafts have been made, but without practical result so far. A tunnel has also been commenced behind the miners' bungalow, which has been driven fifty-four feet, but has not yet reached the reef. A little lower down the hill, we come to the road from the store to the reduction works; opening upon which is a level hitherto known as No. 4, but now named the "Road Tunnel." This has reached a distance of seventy-six feet, and will bend off towards the east, to cut the reef upon

which the ancient miners have been so extensively
working. In short, all down this gorge, the surface
has been deeply cut and turned over.*

Still lower down the almost perpendicular face of
the hill, are some very deep trenches, partly filled
with *débris* of quartz, broken up ages ago. At this
spot, No. 1 Tunnel has been driven about sixty feet,
and a slender branchlet of quartz has been intersected. Here again we must cross-cut to reach the
main reef. This is now to be known as the "Korum-
ber Tunnel." Below this is a tunnel which it has
been deemed advisable to abandon because a more
promising spot has since been found for the work.

Still descending, we reach a new tunnel, driven
on another reef, about two feet thick. But as distance
is gained, the vein is increasing in dimensions. This
is called the "Jungle Tunnel," and has penetrated
twenty feet.

After a rather arduous walk through the heavy
jungle, the commencement of the coffee plantations
is reached. Here is situated Tunnel No. 3, or, as it
will now be called, the "Plantation Tunnel." The
intention is to cut both of the reefs, of which one
has already been intersected, and the driving is continued towards the second. This level has reached

---

* By the term "deeply," in reference to ancient workings, I
mean that there has been something more done than mere surface
scratching. But, of course, nothing to compare with the complete
and systematic work of the modern miner.

160 feet, and driving has been commenced upon the course of No. 1 Reef. It was from this tunnel that the quartz and other stone was taken and submitted for analysis at the Bombay Mint; the result showing that the soil in proximity to the reef is also highly auriferous.

Besides the reefs here described, there are four others upon which operations were to be commenced at once. The first is a fine masterly vein that enters our property from the Phœnix. It appears to be about twelve feet thick at the outcrops, has a bearing north and south, and a westerly dip of about forty-five degrees. Another new reef has been discovered a little to the west of the coffee plantations, high up the mountain-side. A third appears lower down, near a stream that flows from Hadiabetta, and has much the same bearing as the above, and is about two feet and a half wide; whilst the fourth is situated about two miles down the Glenrock river, very near the native village, concerning which more hereafter.

These are some of the results of careful explorations made since my visit, and I doubt not are only the beginning of more important discoveries which will be made when the heavy forest has been more thoroughly explored.

CHAPTER IV.

THE REDUCTION WORKS.

The road to the works—The "Harvey Adit"—A meandering
stream—Waterfalls and pools—The water race—Our river—
Its value to the property—Fuel supply—How many feeders
make one stream—Advantages of combination on the part
of the two companies—The site of the works—Preliminary
difficulties—Surface rights secured—The platforms—The building—A plea for patience—The unforeseen and the unexpected
—Zeal of our workmen—A mental forecast of a busy scene.

THE site chosen for the reduction works may, to-
day, be easily reached, either from Glenrock or from
Mango-Tree Hill. Excellent roads were approach-
ing completion before I left the Wynaad; that
from Glenrock was already in use. On my first
visit to the works I took the route which lead
from the South Indian property. Leaving the
bungalow, and passing along the path near the
entrance to the tunnels, which I have described,
when No. 4 Tunnel is reached, instead of rounding
the hill, the road strikes through the coffee plantations in the hollow; and, crossing a small stream
by means of a plank, bears to the left, round

the lofty hill that forms the boundary between the South Indian property and the Government land. This is the hill that intercepts the view from the bungalow down the centre of the Glenrock Valley. After following this path for about a quarter of a mile, it branches, the upper and right hand path leading to Glenrosa ; the lower, which was the one I now took, descending to the stream.

This stream is one of the principal feeders of the Glenrock river. It is worth while to turn round at this point and look back at the road just traversed. For here may be seen the commencement of a new tunnel ; a deep adit, designed by Mr. Harvey to penetrate a distance of 400 fathoms right under the lofty hill. It gradually ascends until it reaches the two reefs on Mango-Tree Range, and it follows that, when finished, it will be the main outlet, along which all the quartz from those reefs will be sent to the reduction works. In its course it is expected that this adit will intersect two, if not three, other reefs on the South Indian property, not as yet prospected.

As a record of Mr. Harvey's connection with the development of the mining scheme on these estates, this important work has been named the "Harvey Adit." The selection of a point of entrance was, however, unfortunate ; for the ground proved loose, and after driving a short distance, the whole gave in. A new entrance has been started a little higher up,

D

where the ground to all appearance is quite secure. When labour can be spared from other and at present more pressing operations, this work will be pushed on. It, of course, cannot be finished for a considerable time; but when it is done, the scheme for the delivery of the quartz will be complete, and there will be an appreciable saving both of labour and time.

But we must continue our journey if we wish to see the works. Crossing the stream and following its downward course, the path is cut through a jungle of marshy plants, with plenty of fine timber overhead. The descent here by a zigzag path is very steep, and we again reach the stream, which we cross a second time at a point where it is joined by another considerable brook, a chain and a half within the boundary of the South Indian property.

At a distance of fifteen chains down stream, there is a succession of picturesque waterfalls, and deep pools. At this spot the water race will be commenced. It is intended to convey the water, in a large aqueduct, a distance of about a thousand feet to the works, where there will be a perpendicular fall of about 120 feet into the turbines which drive the machinery. At the time I visited the place, the river was at its lowest, and from the volume of water I believe that no apprehensions need be entertained that our water supply will at any time fail us.

I need scarcely tell the reader that a good water supply is one of the most important elements of success in mining in this district. Without water power, the increase in the cost of driving machinery must necessarily be very great. Steam engines require fuel, either coal or wood. Of coal the Wynaad has none; of wood the supply is limited, except in a few estates. The cost of the latter, too, will surely increase as consumption goes on.* Hence the value of a sufficient and constant water supply can scarcely be over-estimated.

There are said to be twelve streams that take their rise in and flow through the South Indian property. And though not one of them in itself has sufficient volume to be of any service for motive-power, yet in combination—and they combine just before crossing the boundary at the head of the Glenrock Valley—they form what I may fairly call a little river with a rapid fall.†

The site of the reduction works is reached from the head of this race by a scramble over boulders of rock and fallen trees, the river dashing in a series

* Fortunately in Glenrock we have about 1800 acres of grand forest, which will become more and more valuable every year. It is no exaggeration to say that its value may equal the whole cost of the estate.

† It will be seen how important it is that the two companies should be worked together. Each is dependent upon the other, and a separation of interest, or even divergence in the system of working, would lead to difficulty, and necessitate vastly increased expenditure by both mines.

of cascades into the narrow gorge at the bottom of the valley. It is so far below and so completely shut in by overhanging foliage, that no glimpse of it can be obtained.

It was no easy task to decide upon the most advantageous site upon which to erect the crushing-mill and reduction works; but the decision once arrived at, rapid progress was made in preparing for the buildings. There had been considerable delay before these operations were commenced, owing to the difficulties experienced in effecting an agreement with the proprietors of the surface rights; for it was necessary to obtain their consent before any of the forest could be cleared for building operations. This obstacle ceased to exist as soon as the company became the owners of the surface, as well as of the mining, rights. And it must be remembered that this great advantage was not secured until the early part of the present year, when for the first time it became possible to begin any important work that was not actual mining.

The site selected is a gently sloping space of open ground, at the edge of a steeper incline, surrounded on all sides with magnificent timber. It was necessary to build two retaining walls upon the lower slope to hold the earth excavated in levelling the upper platform, upon which the heavy batteries will be erected.* A lower platform will thus be formed

* Recent letters advise that heavy floods had damaged these

THE HEAD OF THE RACE, GLENROCK RIVER.

to receive the tables and buddles, where the sulphurets will be caught. At the time I visited the spot, one of these retaining walls had been completed; and the foundation level was almost finished. Indeed the work was proceeding vigorously; plenty of labour was available, and it was estimated that the building itself would be commenced within six weeks, and finished before the end of June; and that the work of erecting the machinery could proceed under cover all through the monsoon.

Here, in England, we look at the map, and see the distance from point to point, and calculate that it should take so many days to convey heavy loads (some of them weighing over two tons) a given distance. But the maps afford no indication whatever of the difficulties arising from the nature of the ground to be traversed. After having been dragged up 4000 feet, all these heavy pieces must be let down 1000 feet or so through dense forest; whilst the incline has to be constructed along the face of an almost perpendicular cliff. Then there are projecting masses of rock which require to be blasted away; to say nothing of the thousands of tons of earth that must be removed in the ordinary construction of such a road. All this has actually been done, and done quickly too.

retaining walls so much that it was determined to trust no longer to an artificial platform, and the whole building was to be erected upon the solid hillside. This will involve a little delay, but will not seriously hinder the completion of the building.

It is astonishing how one's eyes are opened by a visit to the spot and a personal acquaintance with the difficulties that had to be overcome. We are then no longer surprised that crushing had not commenced when three months had barely elapsed since the arrival of the machinery at Calicut.

And further, although it is possible to say that so much has actually been done, it would be idle to imagine that we had overcome every difficulty. Much yet remains to be accomplished. Unexpected accidents may happen; unforeseen contingencies may arise, in spite of the most careful arrangements. I have no desire to damp the ardour of the many who are solicitous for immediate results; but in common fairness, let me plead for patience, and assure all interested in Indian gold-mining, who are not unnaturally eager to see success accomplished, that the men who are on the spot are just as anxious as they are, that their work may soon be completed. But it would be the height of folly to hurry on such work at the risk of its stability. The utmost care is necessary in the preparation of the foundations and the proper setting of the stamping plant. If such work is unduly hastened, it might perhaps have all to be done over again, and the last delay would *then* be far worse than the first.

Standing here on this open space of ground, and watching the busy scene, I could scarcely help drawing upon my imagination, and picturing to myself how it would appear a few months hence, when all these uninteresting preliminaries were finished. I saw, in mental vision, the crushing-house built of iron and wood; the solid iron pillars supporting the roof, constructed in England and sent out so as to be erected with as little delay as possible. Behind the house, again, upon the bank above, are the stone-crushers, from which the broken quartz is conducted into the stamping machinery by a series of shoots. The ore, the picture shows me, is being rapidly delivered into the stone-crushers along two different inclined tramways; the one from the north, from the South Indian mines, a mile and three-quarters away; the other from the south, bringing down the Glenrock quartz. Although reduction will be proceeding under one roof, that roof covers two completely distinct sets of machinery, each consisting of two batteries of ten heads of stamps each. I can therefore imagine them in full work, with the thunder of forty heavy stamps incessantly pounding upon their ponderous anvils. Then I could fancy the two powerful turbines, driven by the column of water falling from a height of 120 feet, and capable of working either independently or together as may be necessary. On the lower platform are the four buddles. In these the semi-liquid mass is being churned and manipulated, so that the heavy particles may be deposited, and the light earthy matter allowed to pass away. What becomes of the concentrates thus saved will be told in another chapter; but if thus I anticipate, yet may the mental excursion be fairly offered to the reader; for this in all probability will be the scene before the close of the present year.

THE SITE OF THE REDUCTION WORKS.

CHAPTER V.

OUR WESTERN BOUNDARY.

An early start—Our escort—Something about the Korumbers—
Majestic timber—" Wait-a-bits," and an experience of their
power—A formidable descent—Clumps of bamboos—A village
of wild men—Another river—Signs of gold—A forest breakfast
—Butterflies—A late return—Reefs hidden in the forest.

I HAVE already mentioned that the Glenrock Valley
comprises about 3100 acres of surface, barely one-
third of which has yet been explored. The un-
explored portion consists mainly of heavy forest and
thick jungle. One of the most arduous expeditions
I undertook during my visit was when, in company
with Messrs. Pinching and Ryan, I visited the ex-
treme western boundary of the estate.

We started from Mango-Tree Bungalow at half-
past five in the morning, taking with us a couple of
coolies to carry our breakfast. Our route was over
the ground described in the preceding chapter as
leading to the reduction works. But when this spot
was reached, we started through a belt of forest, till
we came to the lowest portion of the coffee planta-

tions, at the end of which Mr. Ryan met us, with half a dozen Korumbers, to show us the way.

These men, the Korumbers, are natives of the district, who sometimes, but not often, can be induced to work. They are, unfortunately, a very unsatisfactory class to deal with. Work to them is in no sense pleasure. They are, however, first-rate fellows at such labour as felling trees, and surface work. They are, too, thoroughly familiar with the country, and make the best shikarees, or hunts-men.

Armed with sharp knives and billhooks, this curious escort preceded us, in single file, cutting down the thorns and jungle that had grown across the path, and halting, occasionally, to consult as to the best route to take; for we were now threading our way through thick forest which had no beaten track.

I need hardly say that we frequently stopped to look at the noble trees, rising to an enormous height (in some cases 300 feet), and straight as a ship's mast. Poon spars, worth almost anything could they be got down to the coast; blackwood, so valuable for building purposes; rosewood, and many other species known only under native names. Our progress was necessarily slow, and much hindered by the thousands of young trees growing all over the surface. Care had to be taken, also, lest we should come into contact with the vicious long shoots of a species of calamus, armed with sharp thorns—some-

times, and with singular appropriateness, called
"wait-a-bits."

In this respect, I shall never forget the ludicrous
appearance of a friend of mine who had incautiously
ridden under some trees, from the branches of which
a few shoots of this desperate trailing plant depended.
His solar topee had been caught; and the tearing
noise startled the pony, which unluckily bolted through
the thicket—the result being the complete destruction
of almost every article of clothing my unfortunate
friend had on him.

After proceeding for some distance through the
forest, we came to an enormous mass of rock
towering like a wall high above our heads, with, at
our feet, an exceedingly steep descent. Our road
lay down the latter, and this, we were told, was the
worst part of the journey. Looking at it did not
improve matters; so we set about getting down as
best we could, slipping continually, for the dead
leaves with which the ground was covered afforded
no foothold. Nor was it a very cheering thought
that on our return we must climb this formidable
hill. Safely at the bottom, we found ourselves on
the banks of the Glenrock river; a foaming cascade
over which somehow we managed to scramble, and
then ascended the opposite side through more forest,
in which the splendid timber had given place to fine
clumps of bamboo.

Another mile, and we descended into an open

level space, where the Naiker village is situated. The inhabitants are jungle men, who live on roots and herbs in a worse than semi-state of wildness. The village consists of a few huts, enclosed in a square palisade of bamboo for protection against wild beasts.   Our advent was announced by the barking of the pariah dogs, which seemed to resent our approach; and presently a door opened, and sundry of the inhabitants appeared, whose costume is simplicity itself, being that of pure nature. A fine athletic young man was the spokesman. After some preliminary conversation with our Korumbers, he prepared to conduct us to the end of our journey.

A short distance beyond this village, we arrived at another fine mountain stream, nearly, but not quite so large as the Glenrock river. This stream has its source on the Wentworth estate, some 800 feet, I should say, above us. Here there is volume and fall enough to drive any crushing machinery—a note to be made, for use at some future time. Having crossed, we again ascended through more forest, and about a third of a mile further on found our boundary stone—indicating that we had reached the lowest part of the Glenrock estate on the right bank of the river. On the opposite side, our property extends a short distance still further down.

All about here are enormous outcrops of quartz, and plenty of indications that the natives had found it profitable to crush and wash for gold in their primitive fashion. If I mistake not, we too before long will be following their example, as appearances seem to favour the notion that a fine reef here extends across the river into Glenrock land opposite. A little further, and we reached the end of our morning's excursion; where it was proposed to breakfast and rest for a couple of hours.

It was now nearly ten o'clock, and the sun was very hot. We chose a shady glen on the opposite side of the main river, where the pleasant sound of falling water, the beauty of the surrounding foliage, and the cool shelter of ferny rocks, made just the very spot for a delightful *déjeuner*. Here we take our mid-day siesta, and watch the butterflies as they come trooping down the stream; magnificent creatures, radiant in every brilliant hue, some so large as to measure five or six inches across their outspread wings, others tiny in size but resplendent in colour. And how different their motions! One hurries down, as though he had important business to transact at Nelumboor, and was afraid he would be late. Another, being somewhat undecided, flits by in a hesitating kind of way; whilst a third means pleasure and nothing else—so he hovers lovingly over a cool fern and enjoys himself. One, being of an inquiring turn of mind, settled deliberately upon the sketch I was making, and so fell a victim to his own curiosity. I have frequently observed the partiality of butterflies for falling water, but have never seen such a remarkable and varied flight of these insects as this I now beheld.

We had been four hours coming a distance of as many miles in a straight line. We started on our return a little before one o'clock, and reached home, utterly exhausted, about seven in the evening, having retraced our steps nearly the whole way. Unfortunately, on arriving at the coffee plantations, instead of finding our horses waiting for us, as they should have been according to arrangement, they were nowhere to be seen. We were therefore obliged to climb up to the Glenrock Bungalow, and then ride home on borrowed steeds.

And what, it may be asked, was the practical result of this expedition? We had seen indications of reefs, but had not been able to make any careful explorations. Spots had been noted for further examination; but it was clear that anything like a systematic prospecting of all this portion of the estate would be well nigh impossible, until a path has been cut down to the bottom of the valley, so that our engineers can ride back again after their work. This will be done so soon as coolies can be spared from other and more important operations. Already we hear of one promising reef having been traced, about a quarter of a mile down the stream, within the forest I have described; and upon this, prospecting operations have been commenced. Doubtless others yet remain hidden in the thick jungle, to be brought to light as exploration, which must necessarily be a work of time, proceeds.

Recent letters speak of another massive reef having been found two miles below the reduction works; concerning which, one of our mining captains writes, that it is one of the finest he has ever seen. Operations upon this reef must be deferred until the new road to the western boundary, now being constructed, has been finished.

CHAPTER VI.

THE PROPERTIES AROUND US.

Visit to the Indian Trevelyan—A choice of roads—The Devala
Moyar estate—" Trespassers beware ! "—First sight of " free
gold "—Ancient workings and modern tunnels—Athikanu—
Signs of recent workings of the Korumbers—The Limerick
estate—Site of church and hospital—Our own property at
Bittusal—A promising bit indeed!—Might be worked separately
—The Glenrock Valley—Glenrock proper and Glenrosa
described—On the road to Glenrosa—Works at Glenrosa—A
compact property in itself.

ANOTHER pleasant expedition to the estates, now the
property of the Indian Trevelyan Company, will be
found, I think, worthy of a brief description.

There are two roads to Athikanu from Mango-
Tree Hill. One goes by way of Pundalur, through
Sandhurst and Richmond; the other along the old
road from Cherambadi to Devala. We determined
to go by the one and return by the other.

Riding through Pundalur to the Richmond estate,
two roads are met; that to the right being the road
by which I arrived from Devala. But the left road,
passing the works of the South-East Wynaad Company, was our present route. After a further three

miles along a capital road, we reached the high land overlooking Athikanu ; having on our right the property of the Devala Moyar Company—which, by the way, is now forbidden ground, no one being allowed to cross the boundary.*

A short distance under the comforting shade of large trees, brought us to the temporary bungalow upon Athikanu, where we were met by Captain Morrish and his assistant, who are in charge of the operations. They were evidently not a little proud of their charge ; and showed me a number of pieces of quartz, broken off that morning promiscuously from the outcrops, in which gold appeared in the form of distinct grains. This was the first time I had actually seen free gold in the stone on the spot.

We then proceeded to examine the wonderful remains of old native workings. These are most extensive ; the entire face of the hill, where the reef is exposed, had been quarried out, and the descent to the bottom was along a ridge of loose quartz and *débris*, that had been left after the ancient search for nuggets. All this, I was informed, was still worth putting through the mill, as it contained more than sufficient gold to pay for the working. Near the bottom, Captain Morrish had put in a tunnel, which had reached the reef ; and quantities of beautifully

---

* This prohibition has caused not a little inconvenience to planters and others, who formerly availed themselves of short cuts through these estates. Now they must ride miles round.

white quartz had been heaped at the entrance. This, I noticed, was rich in pyrites, more silvery in appearance than that taken from the South Indian reefs, indicating the presence of a larger quantity of sulphur.

The reef at Athikanu, where it has been struck by our tunnel, is not yet cut through, although more than twenty-five feet thick to the furthest point reached. At the foot of the hill, another level had been begun, which was progressing satisfactorily. Close to hand was the stream which, even at this, the driest period of the year, contained a good supply of water, although I fancy there is scarcely sufficient fall to afford driving power. A little to the east, however, on the adjoining Limerick estate, it would furnish a fall of about sixteen feet.

But to return to Athikanu. Close to this point, we noticed what appeared to be an old river-bed, possibly a former course of the present stream. The gravel and stones were evidently water-worn, and on trying some of it by rough washing, we got a very encouraging show of free gold. Having crossed the stream, and proceeded in a northerly direction over an open level space, surrounded with tolerably large trees, we ascended the gently sloping hill on the opposite side. Immense masses of quartz cover the hill, in all probability indicating the presence of an enormous reef. The Korumbers have apparently found this spot very favourable for their rough opera-

tions; for numerous basin-shaped hollows have been
made on these exposed outcrops, which served them
as mortars, in which they have ground down broken
pieces of quartz; whilst small channels cut in the
ground have supplied them with water for washing.
Here, at any rate, is evidence that gold-mining has
been carried on, even to a recent date; and judging
from the pieces I was shown, these rough operations
must have been tolerably successful.

We next rode through the Limerick estate, and
reached the high road to Devala, in sight of the gap
in the hills where, I was informed, Rhodes Reef is
situated.

Near the lofty Needlerock Peak, close to which
we were now riding, we saw the site of the proposed
new church, the foundations being already in process
of excavation. The hospital is also here. This is
the old Government dispensary. It has recently
been enlarged to afford increased accommodation for
European patients; the expense having been defrayed
by contributions from several of the new mining
companies.

From an elevated point near the hospital, we
had an excellent bird's-eye view over the "Trevelyan" estate, upon which part of that company's
property no mining operations had yet been commenced.

Returning by the road to the north of Athikanu,
we entered the South Indian estates at Bittusal, and

had a look at the tunnel being driven from the road in a southerly direction for the purpose of cutting a reef, supposed to be a continuation of that on the Mango-Tree Range, a mile and a quarter to the west. This tunnel has struck the reef on the north or hanging wall side.

Bittusal is a piece of land, consisting of about twenty-three acres, adjoining the property originally purchased by the South Indian Company, and subsequently acquired by that company at a small cost. It now promises to be a valuable addition, and is being opened out by three tunnels, to one of which I have just alluded as being driven from the north. The other two enter from the opposite side of the hill, upon the face and summit of which there are extensive outcrops, worked by the Korumbers in the same manner as at Athikanu. As yet the reef has not been reached from the south, although one of the tunnels had been driven in 160 feet; for operations are only carried on here, when labour can be spared from the main works on Mango-Tree Hill.

In the valley between Bittusal and the western portion of the Caroline and Adeline estates, there appears to be plenty of fine timber. For the present it will be sufficient to open out these works in preparation for the more serious operation of crushing; yet the distance to the reduction works is so great, that it may perhaps be found more economical to erect a battery of stamps on the spot; or possibly

LOWER GLENROCK VALLEY.

this part of the estate may be taken up for work by a distinct company.

The Glenrock Valley is divided into two portions; the river, which flows through the centre along its entire length, being the boundary between two am-shams; or, as we should say in England, counties.

All the part of the valley upon the left bank of the river known as Glenrock proper is in Munanad Amsham; whilst that on the opposite side is called Glenrosa, which is in Cherankód Amsham. Upon the Glenrosa side mining operations have also been commenced upon a promising series of outcrops. To reach these works from Mango-Tree, the road to the reduction works must be followed, until the point where it divides, just before descending to cross the stream, is reached. From this the upper path, which gradually rises along the face of the lofty hills to our right, leads round the spur of a projecting hill, and we find ourselves above a fine coffee plantation, situated in a smaller valley opening out to the south, and facing Hadiabetta Peak on the opposite side.

Above our heads, we had a sight of Mr. Severn's prospecting trench on Yellambullay, the property of the Indian Gold Mines Company of Glasgow, but now abandoned in favour of more concentrated operations near Devala. A beautiful little stream flows down from the heights above, forming a series of cascades over rocky boulders, and forcing its course down to the Glenrock river, joins it a little

below our reduction works. After crossing the
stream, and skirting the opposite hillside, I observed
immense masses of white quartz, indicating a powerful reef bearing north-north-west and south-south-
east. Here two levels are being driven for the
purpose of cutting this reef. The ground has proved
to be exceedingly hard, and but slow progress can
be made ; but one of these tunnels, now 133 feet in
length, has intersected a thin vein which looks very
well, and it cannot be long before the main reef is
reached. Another tunnel, which has advanced sixty
feet, is also promising soon to reach the reef, which
appears to be lying flatter than was at first anticipated.

A short distance to the west of these outcrops,
there are indications of what is supposed to be a
second reef running in the same direction. A cross-
cut has been commenced from one of the tunnels to
reach this new reef; and should it prove successful,
we shall here have a very compact little property,
with every essential for mining self-contained—reefs,
water, and timber. Of the second there is sufficient
fall and volume for driving ; and unusual facilities
for damming the stream high up, should it be found
desirable to form a reservoir, which I scarcely think
will be necessary.*

From Glenrosa there is a splendid open view of

* It seems to me that Glenrosa might well occupy the attention
of another company, being, as I have said, so well supplied in
essentials and self-contained.

the whole of the lower Glenrock Valley, and a good idea of its extent may be formed from the sketch taken on the spot.

Through the kindness of Mr. Ryan I had an opportunity of visiting the Phœnix estate, which, as I have already mentioned, occupies ground adjoining and to the south of the Glenrock and South Indian properties.

The situation of the possessions of the Indian Phœnix Company is very commanding. The only approach to Glenrock from the high road passes through Rosedell and St. Thomé, a series of rounded hills almost destitute of trees, but which it is believed will be found to contain a good supply of auriferous quartz, at present hidden below the promising outcrops plainly visible on the surface.

Following a footpath across the Rosedell estate, just below Hadiabetta Peak, we entered a considerable scrub wood upon Lytton, where the ground begins to descend rapidly. Thence rounding the spur of a hill to the left, we reached the picturesque waterfall at the head of the Phœnix Valley. On the opposite side of the stream rises the lofty timber-covered range of hills upon the Palmerston estate—now the property of the Indian Consolidated Gold Company—dipping almost precipitously to the water.

About nine hundred yards below the cascade, is the site of their reduction works. The valley narrows to this point, almost becoming a gorge; thence it gradually opens out again, the Phœnix Company possessing the right bank only. Down to the narrowest point there is but little timber; but below there is a fair amount of serviceable forest.

Upon Phœnix, the mining operations proper had been suspended for the moment. The entire force of native labour had been put on the earthworks, roads, and water race, upon which considerable progress had been made; and there is ample evidence that all these very essential operations had been pushed on with highly commendable vigour. In the short time since work has began, a great deal has been done in the way of preparatory operations; and on Mr. Grove's return from Australia he will find his communications open, his platform and foundations ready for the stamping house, the water race tolerably well on; and then, tunnel-driving will doubtless be proceeded with as rapidly as possible. I did not see any bungalows for European assistants, nor did I visit all the outcrops referred to in Mr. Grove's first report. From all that I could learn, a good opinion is held concerning the prospects of the Phœnix Company; and with the energy and skill of their experienced manager they will probably not be far behind their neighbours in showing results.

CHAPTER VII.

THE QUESTION OF LABOUR.

Necessity that labour should be plentiful and cheap—Abundance
offering in the Wynaad—Timidity of the natives—Chinese
immigration considered—The system of imported labour—
Local cultivators—The Korumbers—Principal sources of supply
—Canarese coolies from Mysore—The Moplahs—The Wuddurs
and Balkaras—Payment by advances described—Differences in
the system on various estates—Interest of the gold companies
in the question—Proposed help from Madrasse Eurasians—
Peculiarities of the class—Need of English miners as headmen
—Arrangements of our staff—Necessity of departmental
system and reports.

AMONGST the essentials to success in gold-mining in
this, or, indeed, in any district, not the least important is the question of labour. There may be
gold on the reefs; there may be water sufficient for
driving power; and ample timber for building and
other purposes : but if there is no labour procurable,
or only such as is very costly, it would scarcely be
possible to mine with success. An inquiry as to
labour facilities should not, therefore, be overlooked
in writing on this subject.

Whilst in the Wynaad, my serious attention was

directed to this matter; and I am satisfied that for
all ordinary work, no apprehension need be felt that
the supply of labour will fall short of our requirements. There is a constant flow of native labourers
into the Wynaad for coffee cultivation; and these
very readily take employment in every kind of surface
work, though as yet not many care to undertake
underground labour. Amongst the few who will do
it, it is exceptional to find men physically capable
of the severe exertion entailed by the use of the pick
upon hard rock.

So far no accident has happened through the
falling in of any of the tunnels. It is not pleasant
to contemplate the probable consequences of such
an accident. The native of India is naturally timid,
and is also reluctant to attempt work to which he is
unaccustomed. Should unexpected dangers be en-
countered, he would in all likelihood stubbornly
refuse to enter a tunnel again. This is a contingency
which should be provided against. On the other
hand, as has often been said of native soldiers, the
men are bold and daring when well led. It follows
that when encouraged by the example of good
European miners, they will soon gather courage and
develop into useful workmen—though it must be
admitted that any ordinary Cornish miner would be
able to do the work of three natives. It is, therefore, a prime necessity to provide a good staff of
miners, who have been accustomed to underground

labour and timbering; for of this part of a miner's work the native has not the slightest idea.

It has been suggested that as Chinamen are first-rate workmen, having excellent points in their favour, it would be advantageous to encourage Chinese immigration. Under some circumstances this might be a good course to adopt. Yet I venture to think that in Southern India it would not prove of benefit in the long run. Any considerable influx of Chinese workmen would in all probability exercise an unfavourable influence upon native labour. I have already said that native labour is both abundant and cheap. It would, therefore, be unwise to introduce a hostile element likely to discourage, and perhaps entirely divert, the stream of labour now beginning to flow into the district. Of course it is quite impossible to predict what would be the consequence of such an experiment. I simply express my opinion for what it is worth; and it is, that the introduction of Chinese labour would be, for the reasons I have shown, a dangerous experiment.

It should be well understood that, as a district, the Wynaad is very thinly populated, and, speaking in general terms, it is not from inhabitants on the spot that the labour is derived for coffee cultivation. The labourers are mostly brought from considerable distances by contractors, or, as they are called, *maistrees*, who enter into agreements beforehand with the planters for the services of their gangs. As a rule, local labourers will belong to one or other of the following clans or tribes: Naïkers, Burgurs, or Korumbers; the immigrants will be Canarese, Moplahs, Wuddurs, and Bālkaras.

The first—*Naïkers*—are jungle men, who can scarcely be induced to work, and then only very spasmodically.

Burgurs are local cultivators, who will sometimes come and do a few days' work, when not engaged at their own villages. They also can scarcely be depended upon.

The *Korumbers* make the best foresters; but like all such roving tribes, they are an unsatisfactory class to deal with; and will never do manual work, if they can possibly help it. They are not usually cultivators of the soil, but are invaluable on account of their thorough knowledge of the country. Their observation, in truth, is so keen that they can tell the position of every outcrop of quartz in the place. The Korumbers have always been gold-miners in a desultory sort of a way; washing in river-beds, breaking up boulders in their search for the precious metal, working singly or in small parties, in the method I shall describe in the next chapter. They are consequently most useful in prospecting over jungle-covered country.

The principal source of the labour supply is Mysore. From it come large gangs of *Canarese coolies*, who are hardy and intelligent workmen, easily taught, and having no caste prejudices. They require some little coaxing to get them underground for the first time ; but they soon acquire confidence. Men, women, and children, all work ; the men getting about four annas a day, and the women two annas and a half. They will undertake any kind of labour, and will ultimately prove very serviceable in reduction works. They will stay some eight or nine months in the district, and will then want to go home.

The *Moplahs* belong to several tribes of the Malabar coast, where they are in a condition of semi-slavery to the landowners and wealthier men of their villages. I was informed that they are greatly oppressed, and glad when they can manage to escape from this state of bondage. There is some hope that these people will ultimately migrate in a body to the Wynaad. At present they only stay a few weeks, and are, therefore, seldom taken on, except in emergencies. They are not better labourers than the Canarese ; but have secured a higher tariff of pay, as they get five annas a day.*

Two other classes of labourers deserve mention. The *Wuddurs*, or earth contractors and stone workers. These men come from the Malabar side below the Ghâts. They will not touch timber, and are never

* The gentleman from whom I received these particulars has been a resident in the Wynaad for many years, and is thoroughly familiar with the natives who are employed in the district.

engaged by the day, doing the work by contract. The *Bālkaras*, from the same district, are, on the other hand, sawyers by occupation, and only work with timber.

The system of advances which prevails in the Wynaad is not altogether satisfactory. In short, opinions differ widely as to the best mode of dealing with native labour in the matter of pay. The maistree, or contractor, who receives an advance of perhaps two or three hundred rupees, engages to bring up a gang of coolies by a certain time, and keep them together. He receives a commission of ten per cent. of the wages earned. On some estates the coolies are paid weekly in full; usually on Saturday, as Sunday is bazaar day at Devala.

The commission is not paid to the contractor, but placed to his credit as against the advance originally paid to him, which is thus gradually worked off. When the term for which he has contracted has been completed, the account is squared, either by payment of the balance due to him, or by receiving from him the balance of his advance which has not been earned by commission. He is then at liberty to enter into a fresh agreement, receiving a further advance. But many planters find it the best policy to pay the commission weekly, when they pay the coolies—treating the sum originally advanced as a permanent deposit; the contractor understanding that he is expected to keep up the supply of labour from season to season.

THE JUNGLE TUNNEL, GLENROCK.

This plan, I am told, works very well; for losses but seldom occur. The maistrees as a class may be thoroughly depended upon.

Upon some estates the coolies are not paid in full at the close of each week, for a small sum is kept back from each week's pay until the end of the term, when they are paid up. The coolie is thus sent away with a tolerably fair amount of savings, and goes back to his village in a position to add another piece of land to his home, or to buy some additional copper vessels—those vessels so dearly prized. The idea is, that finding such substantial benefit resulting from his labour, the coolie is the more ready to return and earn more. On the other hand, the advocates of full payment on every Saturday contend that every coolie will spend as much as he can get; and finding at the close of his engagement he has nothing to carry home with him, goes on working from sheer necessity, because actually living from hand to mouth. There can be no doubt which course is the best for the coolie, but planters have their own opinions as to the system they think most advantageous to themselves.

I have examined that the pay of a first-class coolie would be two annas a day. A Cornish timberman will draw £10 per month, besides the heavy expense that must be incurred in sending him out to India. His daily wage will, therefore, be about Rs. 7, 6a., or nearly twenty-four times as much as that of an able-bodied native labourer. Remembering

THE JUNGLE TUNNEL, GLENROCK.

This plan, I am told, works very well; for losses but seldom occur. The maistrees as a class may be thoroughly depended upon.

Upon some estates the coolies are not paid in full at the close of each week, for a small sum is kept back from each week's pay, until the end of the term, when they are paid up. The coolie is thus sent away with a tolerably fair amount of savings, and goes back to his village in a position to add another piece of land to his home, or to buy some additional copper vessels—those vessels so dearly prized. The idea is, that finding such substantial benefit resulting from his labour, the coolie is the more ready to return and earn more. On the other hand, the advocates of full payment on every Saturday contend that every coolie will spend as much as he can get; and finding at the close of his engagement he has nothing to carry home with him, goes on working from sheer necessity, because actually living from hand to mouth. There can be no doubt which course is the best for the native, but planters have their own opinions as to the system they think most advantageous to themselves.

I have mentioned that the pay of a first-class coolie would be five annas a day. A Cornish timber-man will draw £16 per month, besides the heavy expense that must be incurred in sending him out to India. His daily wage will, therefore, be about Rs. 7, 6*a*., or nearly twenty-four times as much as that of an able-bodied native labourer. Remembering

this great disproportion of cost, and taking into con-
sideration, on the other hand, the greater advantage
accruing from the employment of skilled and experienced workmen, it will readily be admitted that
the interests of a mining corporation must be bound
up in the encouragement and education of native
labour; which, considering its abundance and cheap-
ness, will necessarily be the best for all kinds of
work, except actual operations on the solid reef. And
even at such work some few of the Canarese coolies
are beginning to show aptitude that promises well in
the future. It is clearly, therefore, a good policy to
select such men from the rest and pay them higher
wages as an encouragement. If this be done, I have
no doubt that, in time, a better class of workmen
will be attracted to the mines; and so the present
difficulty will disappear.

I should not omit to say, here, that an attempt is
being made to find employment for Madrasse
Eurasians, or lads of mixed parentage. Their services
may be obtained at from Rs. 25 to Rs. 30 per month;
but as a class, Eurasians have hitherto not shown
much disposition to undertake hard manual labour.
They are too often addicted to the vices of drink and
improvidence; and as long as they have money to
spend, it is spent in the manner most likely to
render them unfit for work. This failing is well
known to all who have had experience of them.
Indeed, within the last few years, an association has

been formed in Madras for the purpose of encouraging a healthier tone amongst the poorer Eurasian lads. It is hoped that by bringing proper influence to bear upon them, they may be induced to lay aside their class prejudices against hard work, and practise sobriety. For those who hold out promise that reform will be permanent, employment is found, and their career watched with interest. The recommendation of this society should have weight with employers, who are thus guarded against taking into their service men who would, in all probability, not be worth their salt. Of course it will be understood that I am speaking only of the poorest of the Eurasian population of Madras; the class from which alone such labour is likely to be drawn.

Experienced European miners will always be necessary, in order to take the lead, and educate by their example the natives, who, it must be remembered, will necessarily always form the bulk of the working staff. Stress must be laid upon *example.* The men sent out should clearly understand that their duty will be work, and not supervision. This latter is a mistaken idea that not unfrequently possesses them. I have had considerable experience in dealing with the natives of India in various descriptions of work, and I unhesitatingly say that the power of *example* has succeeded when every other course must have failed utterly. Upon this principle, the true value of the English miner will be found to

F

consist in the moral influence he will exercise over the native who sees him actually doing the very duty which he, the native, is expected to do.

Under the general manager, who has the entire oversight and direction of the operations in all the different departments, whose duty it is so to manage that the whole machine works easily and harmoniously, there will be the superintendents of the various sections; a mining captain in more immediate charge of each distinct group of operations; a chief engineer responsible for the machinery; a reduction officer to conduct the reducing works; a surveyor; a surface superintendent; and an accountant—all of whom should report periodically to the manager. And these departmental reports should be forwarded by him, with his own remarks, to the board of directors at home.

CHAPTER VIII.

THE PROCESS OF REDUCTION.

The process not easy—German theory—English practical experiences—Variety in the latter—Recent new patents—The elephant stamp—Its advantages if serviceable—Our batteries—Crushing—Extraction by quicksilver—Final processes—Delicate operations—In the crucible at last !—Necessity of skill and care—Precautions necessary against *loss* of gold—The native process of washing—Its bearing upon reputed assays—How an assay should be made.

The extraction of the precious metals from the quartz, or other mineral in which they may be held (or, as it is technically called, the *matrix*), is by no means so simple an operation as many seem to imagine. As a matter of fact, it involves a number of complicated and difficult questions, regarding which various authorities differ in opinion upon almost every point of detail. Most of the best writings on the subject of the reduction and concentration of gold are by German authors. English experts have obtained their experience either in Australia, California, or Brazil, and in each of these countries they have worked under different conditions. The result of this variety has been to make them biased in favour of those processes and systems of machinery which have been found to succeed best in the locality where they have operated.

Now, India is an entirely new field, and it is, therefore, still a matter of great uncertainty which of the various systems recommended will be found the best for adoption in it.

As with all new industries, so it has been with gold reduction—the establishment of important gold-mining companies within the past two years has attracted the attention of manufacturing engineers in this country, and new patents are continually being pressed on the notice of directors. These offer alleged improvements in stone crushing, in stamping, in concentrating, which look promising enough on paper, but are hitherto untried, and may only manifest their defects when brought to the test of actual practice.

The old Australian gravitation batteries have been in operation for many years, and are known to have answered satisfactorily, but they are immensely heavy and very costly.

The new elephant stamps are highly recommended in some quarters. As yet, however, these latter must still be considered on their trial. Some of the new Indian companies have adopted them, and we may hope soon to hear about their capabilities. They have some manifest advantages over the gravitation stamps. Being much lighter, they are easily moved from place to place. They require less motive power, and their first cost is considerably less. All these things are strongly in their favour ; and if in actual operation they prove to be as serviceable as their advocates contend, they will doubtless be a valuable acquisition. But this result is exactly what has yet to be demonstrated.

The crushing machinery sent out by the South Indian and Indian Glenrock Companies, consists of eight batteries, of five gravitation stamps each, in all, forty heads of stamps. These have been manufactured by Messrs. Appleby Brothers of East Greenwich, at a cost of about £6000, the total weight being over 190 tons.

I now propose briefly to describe the processes of reduction. The quartz, after having been broken up in the stone crushers, passes into the stamp coffers or mortars, where it is stamped in water to the degree of fineness requisite to liberate the particles of gold from their natural matrix. This being done, the object of all the subsequent operations is to separate and secure these golden particles from the worthless matter or tailings. This is accomplished in all cases by the use of quicksilver, and various methods are adopted for this purpose. The three principal systems, upon one or other of which, or upon modifications or combinations of the same, all gold-reducing machinery is designed, may be described as follows :—

I. Quicksilver is introduced into the stamp boxes. Then, as the pulp issues from the mortar, it is made to pass through troughs containing mercury, and over amalgamated copper plates, or ripples, so as to arrest the particles of gold on their way from the stamps.

II. The same as above, only no mercury is used in the mortar boxes. In these cases, all the amalgamation is performed outside the batteries, by passing the pulp through mercury troughs and over amalgamated plates, and other devices to gain the gold.

III. The pulp is not allowed to come into contact with quicksilver, until it has been concentrated up to from four to six to the hundred, by means of blankets or skins, the fibres of which arrest the sand and metallic particles on their way as a stream over tables or strakes, which latter are set at an angle of one to twelve to one to sixteen, according to circumstances. In connection with these blanket tables, I should add that, in order to afford a final chance of recovering as large a percentage as possible of the very finest particles that the blankets have failed to retain, buddles are employed, so as further to impoverize the tailings.

The concentrates from the blankets and buddles may then be introduced, with the necessary quantity of quicksilver, into strong barrels, which are kept revolving from eighteen to twenty-four hours. When discharged, the amalgam separates from the sand,

and as much as possible of the superfluous quicksilver is pressed out of it through wash-leather; the remaining quicksilver being expelled by heat from the retorts in which the amalgam is placed.

The sulphurets which have been retained in the concentrates are often submitted to a process called chlorination. The principle of this is the alleged property possessed by chlorine gas of changing gold into a chloride. This process consists in first roasting the sulphurets, to drive off the sulphur, etc., and then, when cool, damping it. It is now placed in an air-tight vessel of peculiar construction, into which the chlorine gas is admitted beneath the pulpy mass to be chlorinized. An escape hole is left at the top of this receptacle, so that, as the gas rises, the common air is expelled, until the vessel is full of chlorine gas, when the hole is stopped, and the contents left undisturbed for twenty-four hours. The next process is to extract the chloride of gold by the introduction of water; and the precious fluid is then drawn off with care into a precipitating vat, where, by the addition of a solution of sulphate of iron, the gold is precipitated, and afterwards easily collected, dried, and melted in a crucible.

All this will sufficiently show that skill and care are necessary to render gold-mining and extraction a success. In proportion as the reduction staff know their business, and attend to it with constant diligence, so will results be satisfactory, or other-

wise. The vital question that must be ever kept
before them, is not so much the quantity of gold
saved, as the quantity *lost;* and with every care
there must always be some loss, which is ascertain-
able by frequent assay of the tailings. The reduction
officer's efforts must therefore be directed to render
this percentage of loss as small as possible. He
cannot help the quartz being poor ; but if he finds
his tailings show gold on assay, he knows at once
that there must be something defective, either in
his machinery or his management. There is then
but one thing to do—to spare no pains to discover
where the weak point is, and, if possible, to remedy it.

I have more than once mentioned the Korumbers ;
and I cannot better conclude this chapter than by a
description of their (the native) method of washing
for gold.

The operation, as practised by them, is exceedingly simple. They use a slightly hollowed wooden
tray of an oval shape. On this tray they place a
few handfuls of finely powdered quartz or earth, and
pouring in water sufficient to cover it, they work the
tray and its contents in a circular direction until the
lighter earthy particles float round with the water,
whilst all heavier grains—the gold, of course, with
the rest—sink to the bottom. When this has been
done sufficiently long, with a sudden and peculiar
jerk, the water is thrown away, whilst the heavier
sediment is retained. The tray is again filled with

water, and the process is repeated; and so on until but a little blackish sand is left behind. Then more crushed quartz is put in, and the operation begins as before. This process is repeated again and again. Each time the sediment becomes richer and richer, until it is determined to finish the operation, and get rid of as much of the sand as possible.

The tray now requires more delicate handling. Less water is used; and that is poured in gently upon a slope. The lighter particles are thus carefully washed to the edge, and brushed out with the hand, every grain being visible. After this washing has been continued for some time there remains but a very little sediment, and this contains the gold. The fact is at once rendered apparent, by tilting the tray and permitting a little water to trickle slowly over the contents. The particles will move gently towards the edge, and the gold, being the heaviest, will be the last to move, and will soon appear as a yellow rim at the top border of the sediment. The Korumbers work very roughly; and I am satisfied that they lose a great deal of the precious metal that would be taken up by the quicksilver in our modern and more delicate process. Besides which, the gold sometimes exists in the form of film, as fine as gold-leaf, and this will float on the surface of the water, and is, therefore, liable to be washed away.

It is necessary to understand this operation of washing, because wrong conclusions may very easily be formed in reading the reports of assayists, through misconception of the nature of the samples submitted for analysis. By way of example, supposing that the residue left in the dish, or tray, after washing down some eight pounds weight of crushed quartz, may not weigh more than a quarter of an ounce. Of course this quarter of an ounce will contain the gold washed out of the original eight pounds. Now the assay report is usually given on the sample submitted; and is not of the remotest use in forming a judgment on the value of a reef, or deposit, unless the proportion that the residue bears to the bulk is also known. What would the Glenrock shareholders have understood by the assay of the sample brought home by me when told that it afforded 555 ounces to the ton? The question here is per ton of what? of quartz, or of the sample?

Now, this particular sample may have been very thoroughly reduced, and its auriferous character will entirely depend on the manner in which it has been washed. In order to find the true quantity of gold in the quartz, it will be necessary to divide the yield of gold afforded in the sample by the proportion the sediment left bore to the entire quantity washed. And the 555 ounces to the ton, then, shows the true quantity of gold to the ton of quartz to be about eighteen pennyweights. Yet, assuming that some gold had been lost in the washing, I next, in order to test the accuracy of the first assay, submitted a quantity of *unreduced* quartz powder, upon which the return made was 1·2 ounce of gold to the ton of quartz—a result that may be considered most satisfactory.

CHAPTER IX.

A FINAL WORD.

Climate of the Wynaad—European comforts—Our church and our doctor—Apathy of the Government—Enterprise of the companies —Want of banking facilities—Necessity of a railway, and resulting advantages—An excuse for unfrequency of official reports—Farewell.

AND now my task draws to a conclusion, and I must say a final word or two on three matters: the climate; the means of communication; and the misconception by many at home of the extent of the difficulties companies have to contend with—the immediate cause of much seemingly unnecessary delay.

In climate the Wynaad will compare favourably with that of almost any part of India, and is infinitely preferable to the climate in many centres of European trade. Except during two months of the year—the middle of March to the middle of May—the district is tolerably free from fever. The monsoon, or rainy season, begins at the end of May and lasts till the end of October; the rainfall is very heavy, but it is not anticipated that mining work will be much hindered. Surface operations, such as road-

MANGO TREE BUNGALOW, FROM GLENROCK.

making and building, must, however, at this time, be suspended ; but where the work is carried on under cover, as in tunnels and reduction buildings, no stoppage is expected. From November to March the weather is bright and pleasant, the atmosphere pure and clear ; and a fine breeze coming from the western coast, makes residence on the Wynaad plateau agreeable enough. In the valleys it will necessarily always be warm. The bungalows are usually built so as to get the full benefit of this breeze.

Fever, to which natives as well as Europeans are subject, is not often fatal in its effects. It arises from the malarious vapours generated by heat on the Terrai, a low swampy ground at the foot of the Ghâts. A liberal use of quinine, as a preventive rather than a cure, is recommended ; but a change to Ootacamund· is the best remedy. So soon as the rains commence, fever disappears ; and with ordinary precautions of moderation in living, especially in the use of spirits, plenty of outdoor exercise, and regularity of habit, no one need fear the effects of the climate. As yet living is somewhat expensive in the Wynaad, though not more so than in many other parts of India. Supplies of European preserved provisions can be obtained at Ootacamund, and even at Guadalur, where an enterprising Parsee merchant has opened a store. Indeed, I understand that he contemplates establishing a branch shop in the new station of Pundalur, which is likely to be a great convenience.

Vegetables, fish, and fruit are forwarded twice a week from Ootacamund by private arrangement, and local dealers afford a very tolerable supply of butchers' meat. Bread is procurable at Devala, though not of good quality. A clever baker would soon make a fortune here. So, on the whole, miners and coffee planters are not so badly off for the good things of this life, as might be supposed. And as the European population of the district increases, trade facilities will also increase, and the demand will create the supply. Itinerant dealers even now ply their trade from estate to estate, and make a very good thing out of sales of tailoring stuffs and other wares.

The Wynaad is as yet entirely without a church, but steps are being taken to provide this want. A site has been selected on the road between Devala and Cherambadi, not far from the Trevelyan and Provident estates. Mr. John W. Ryan is endeavouring to raise the necessary funds, and is taking a deep interest in the practical carrying out of his scheme for the benefit of a growing European population; which will undoubtedly be all the better for his labours.

Medical advice is obtainable at the Government Dispensary, which is open to all; but, in consequence of the great increase in the European population, this useful institution is scarcely equal to the strain now put upon it. A Medical Board has, however, now been formed in London, composed of representatives of five or six companies, who have associated themselves together to send out a fully qualified medical officer, who will be thoroughly conversant with every form of tropical ailment, to take charge of the employés of the companies so associated. This Board also proposes to build and maintain a central hospital and convalescent home, and in other ways to promote the welfare of the combined staffs ; and it is hoped that the results will be satisfactory to all concerned.

We are as yet in the very infancy of this new and promising industry, which, if at all successful, will assuredly be to India one of the greatest benefits it is possible to imagine. But the country will owe its enrichment to private enterprise alone. Years ago, the attention of Government was directed to the circumstance that the Wynaad was full of gold-bearing reefs, but nothing was done. Reports were sent in, duly filed, and put away. Even now, when so much English capital has been subscribed to work these reefs, the Indian Government manifests but little interest in what is going on. The utmost that the pressure brought to bear on the authorities has been able to effect, has been the establishment of a post-office at Pundalur, and a few trifling repairs to some of the bridges in the Malabar district.

It is a true saying that nothing succeeds like success; and we must wait and fight against the numerous drawbacks inseparable from such a wild country, without any friendly assistance from Government. When, in spite of all difficulties, gold begins to be produced, we may perhaps hope for a telegraph station nearer than Ootacamund, forty miles away; and even a bank, that will not be allowed, although a Government treasury, to charge a discount of $\frac{3}{4}$ per cent. for cashing currency notes. We shall no longer be amazed at the sight of a half-naked coolie, trudging along the forty miles of road, with two or three thousand rupees in a canvas bag on his head, with neither peon nor policeman in charge. How it is that specie remittances, thus openly carried across the country, so invariably come to hand in order, is a marvel. But we can scarcely doubt that when the district becomes more civilized, it will not be as safe as it is now.

Then as to the roads. Anywhere else, a railway would have been started long before now. English capital would readily be forthcoming, if a guarantee of four per cent. were offered by the Government. Such a railway, connecting the southern lines with the Mysore branch, would tap a most important district, and secure abundant traffic. There is a continual stream of labour pouring southwards from Mysore, and eastwards from the coast. The entire food supply is drawn from Mysore. The coffee must go down to the coast. Stores, machinery, tools, etc., must go up to the Wynaad. The Ghâts are to-day crowded with trains of bullock-waggons all through the season. How a railway would open up the country! What a necessity it is! It would increase the traffic; traders would then venture to settle on the place; other industries would spring up in all directions; and the Wynaad, from being a desolate and thinly inhabited, and, except for coffee, an unproductive district, would rapidly develop into one of the busiest centres of trade in the whole peninsula. We may live to see accomplished here changes such as, within the memory of the present generation, have been witnessed in California and Australia.

In conclusion, I must refer to the unreasonable eagerness which is often displayed for frequent information from the mines. It is not unnatural that those who are interested in the industry should become impatient when either no report whatever, or only very meagre paragraphs in the mining journals, reach them. But it must not be supposed that, because there is nothing fresh to say, the work is slackened or suspended. At the present stage of operations all that can be reported is that such levels, or roads, have advanced so many feet, or such outcrops have been tried and found auriferous. We are now in the most uninteresting phase of mining, and cannot expect to be striking new reefs every week.

Nevertheless, whilst a manager may have but little to report that proprietors would care to hear, a great deal of heavy work has probably been accomplished; and the day when all this work will tell is being brought so much the nearer. But to the management in England all these dry and uninteresting details are of much importance. For they enable them to follow every operation closely, and form a truer notion of the work that is going on; to anticipate future requirements in men and material; and to place themselves in a position to give trustworthy information when required.

With this explanation to many who, like myself, are deeply interested in our Indian property, but who, unlike me, have not been able to see it for themselves, I have done. I can only hope that my little book may afford them one tithe of the pleasure which the personal inspection of our properties, and association with those who work for us abroad, afforded me.

THE END.

PRINTED BY WILLIAM CLOWES AND SONS, LIMITED, LONDON AND BECCLES